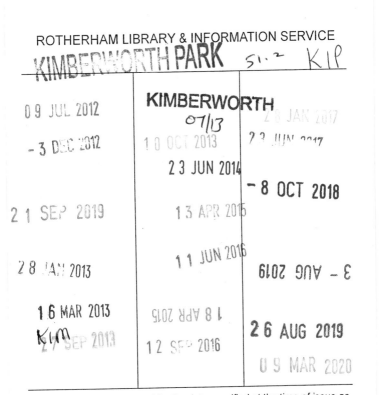

I've been through an incredible journey and I'm proud to say that I shared it with family, friends, Luke and everyone else who I met along the way. E.R.

For Suzanne, Chris, Hannah, Katharine, Lauren
and all at Macmillan. L.M.

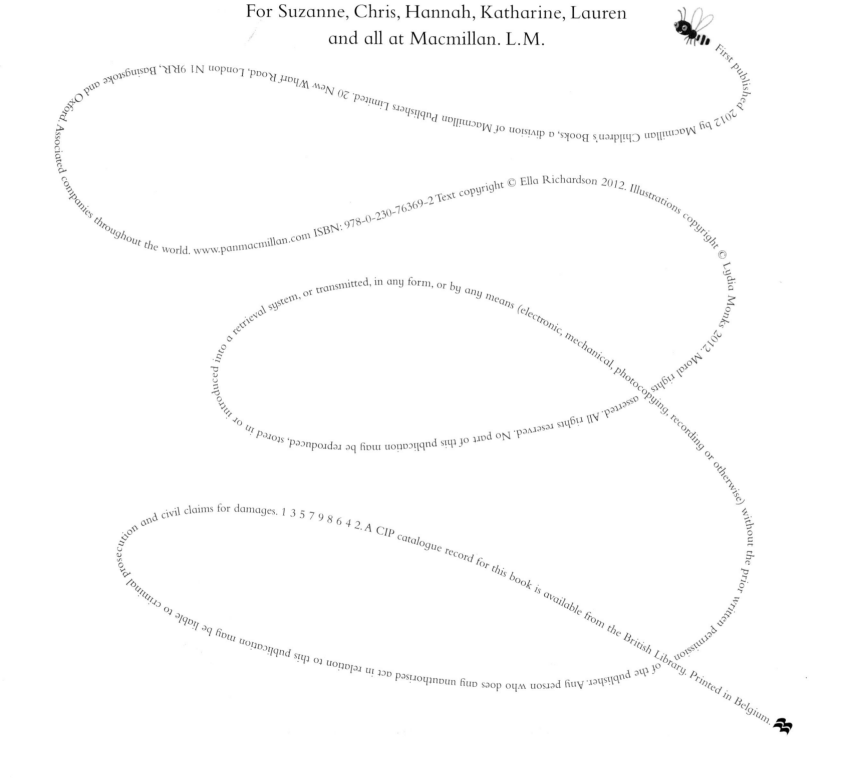

First published 2012 by Macmillan Children's Books, a division of Macmillan Publishers Limited. 20 New Wharf Road, London N1 9RR, Basingstoke and Oxford. Associated companies throughout the world. www.panmacmillan.com ISBN: 978-0-230-76369-2 Text copyright © Ella Richardson 2012. Illustrations copyright © Lydia Monks 2012. Moral rights asserted. 1 3 5 7 9 8 6 4 2. A CIP catalogue record for this book is available from the British Library. Printed in Belgium.

The Bear and the Bees

Written by
Ella Richardson

Illustrated by
Lydia Monks

MACMILLAN CHILDREN'S BOOKS

Our story begins with your imagination!

Now, imagine a world full of black and yellow creatures that fly above your heads.

Bees, yes, but not normal bees.

These bees can talk. And not only can they talk, but they also go to school!

Now this world may be unique in itself, but the creatures living in it aren't so unique.

Actually, they are all EXACTLY the same as each other! And all of these buzzing bees have the same name too. They are all called Bizzy. Every single one of them.

Imagine being in school when the teacher takes the register if you all have the same name? How would you know when it's your name being called out? How confusing would that be? Well, that's what happens to these bees every day.

One ordinary Monday, the younger bees were gathered in the playground. Some were buzzing with the latest gossip, while others played hide and buzz.

All of a sudden, a big brown, hairy creature
strolled into the playground. It was a bear!
The bees buzzed loudly and flew here
and there in a panic.

"Hey guys," the bear spoke softly. "My name is Gruzzle.
Don't be afraid – it's my first day here."

The bees stared in shock at the bear.

"This isn't the right school for you!"
one bee buzzed crossly.

"You're different! You don't have stripes
like us and I bet you can't fly," a second
bee argued.

"And he's not even called Bizzy!" a third
bee joined in. "We don't like people who
are different. Go away!"

Gruzzle's face fell. "Does it matter if I'm
different?" he asked.

The answer was obviously yes, because
the bees flew away into their classrooms,
ignoring his question.

Giant tears fell from Gruzzle's giant eyes and splashed onto the playground.

But one bee had stayed behind – the smallest bee in the whole school.
Comforting Gruzzle, the bee spoke. "There, there! I think it's a good idea,
being different. It's boring when everyone's the same."

Gruzzle smiled as the kind little bee gave him an idea.

The rest of the day zoomed past. Some of the bees made nasty remarks as Gruzzle walked by and giggled behind his back, but Gruzzle didn't care. He had a plan, a good one too. All he needed was imagination, which he sure had already.

The next day, the bees gathered in the playground as normal . . . but then Gruzzle strolled in!

He looked very different from the day before. He had yellow and black stripes painted on him, and had wings tied to his back.

The crowd went quiet and glanced at one another. Then one young bee piped up. "You look so stupid!" he said. "Bears don't have wings," shouted another bee, "and your stripes look silly!"

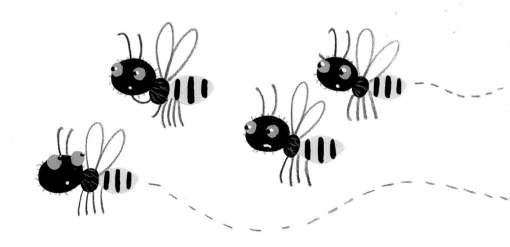

Everyone laughed but they soon stopped as Gruzzle started chuckling too.
"You laughed at me because I'm different," he said, "but when I look the
same as you, you still laugh at me. I AM different, and I'm happy being
a bear. There's nothing wrong with being different!"

The bees paused for a moment, and thought about what Gruzzle had just said. Then the smallest bee started cheering and shouted, "Hurrah for Gruzzle!"

"I'd like to be different,"
a big bee said.
"I'm going to go purple!"

"And I'm going to change
my name to Buzzle,"
another exclaimed.

The next morning, the playground was more cheerful than it had ever been. All the bees were brightly coloured and were buzzing about, trying to learn the new names they had each given themselves.

Gruzzle looked around and smiled. He thought to himself
that it is okay to be unique . . . it's okay to be you!